FORESTHILL
AUG 2017

EMMA'S CIRCUS

Candace Fleming
Pictures by Christine Davenier

MARGARET FERGUSON BOOKS

Farrar Straus Giroux

New York

Last fall my family and I rode into town.

And—I'm not kidding—you know what we saw?

A circus parade just finishing up on Main Street.

"Oh, please," I begged. "We missed the parade. Can we go to the circus?"

But Daddy shook his head and said, "No. There are too many chores to be done on the farm."

"True," said Mama, sighing. "Still, a sword swallower would have been a sight to see."

"And the lions," added Granny dreamily. "I've always loved lions."

"I've never even seen a circus," said my big brother, Sam.

"Me neither," I sniffled.

Daddy put his arm around me. "Sorry, Emma," he said, "but with winter coming there's just no time for a circus."

I turned away. I tried not to cry. And that's when I spied a circus bear on a unicycle.

And this is the truth—I pinky swear—that bear winked . . . at *me*!

The very next morning, the bear pedaled into my yard.

"Look, Daddy, look!" I cried.

But he was too busy picking to pay me any mind.

So my new friend and I played in the barn all day
until Mama hollered, "Supper!"

Then the bear hopped on his unicycle and headed
away down the lane.

"Goodbye," I called after him. "Come back soon."

And—I'm telling no fib—the very next morning, that bear did.

This time he brought along two seals with gold horns.

"Look, Mama, look!" I cried.

But she was too busy canning to pay me any mind.

So my friends and I played in the barn all day
until Mama again hollered, "Supper!"

Then the bear hopped on his unicycle, the seals tooted their
horns, and they all headed away down the lane.
"Goodbye," I called after them. "Come back soon!"

And—I'm not pulling your leg—the very next morning, they did.

This time they brought along three juggling monkeys.

"Look, Granny, look!" I cried.

But she was too busy quilting to pay me any mind.

So my friends and I played in the barn all day
until Mama once more hollered, "Supper!"

Then the bear hopped on his unicycle, the seals tooted their horns, the monkeys juggled their hoops, and they all headed away down the lane.

"Goodbye," I called after them. "Come back soon!"

And—cross my heart—the very next morning, they did.

This time they brought along four knock-kneed camels.

"Look, Sam, look!" I cried.

But he was too busy chopping to pay me any mind.

So my friends and I played in the barn all day
until—you guessed it—Mama hollered, "Supper!"

Then the bear hopped on his unicycle, the seals tooted
their horns, the monkeys juggled their hoops, the camels spat,
and they all headed away down the lane.

"Goodbye," I called after them. "Come back soon!"

And—this is the downright truth—the very next morning, they did.

This time they brought along five lions, six acrobats,

seven sword swallowers, eight elephants, nine clowns, and a

ten-piece brass band.

"Look, everyone, look!" I cried.

But my family was too busy working to pay me any mind.

So my friends and I played in the barn all day until—

Daddy flung open the doors.

"What's going on in here?" he asked.

That was my cue.

"Ladies and gentlemen, children of all ages, step right up

to see the amazing, the incredible—

"EMMA'S CIRCUS!"

The band gave a drumroll and …

My friends and I played, like we had every day,
until the last note of music faded away.

Clapping like crazy, my family leaped to their feet.

"Did you see the sword swallowers?" exclaimed Mama.

"What a sight!"

"And the lions," squealed Granny. "I loved the lions."

"By golly, that was the best circus I've ever seen,"

whooped Sam.

"That was the *only* circus you've ever seen," said Daddy. He grinned. "I sure am glad Emma had time for it."

I bowed.

Then the bear and the seals and the monkeys and the camels and everyone else packed up their things. They all headed away down the lane.

"Goodbye," my family and I called after them.

"Come back soon!"

And would you believe it?

1 BEAR

2 SEALS

5 LIONS

They

7 SWORD SWALLOWERS

8 ELEPHANTS

3 MONKEYS

4 CAMELS

did!

6 ACROBATS

10-PIECE BRASS BAND

9 CLOWNS

For Eric —C.F.

For Uncle John Martini and Aunt Carol
Munder, who took my little Josephine
to a great circus —C.D.

Farrar Straus Giroux Books for Young Readers
An imprint of Macmillan Publishing Group, LLC
175 Fifth Avenue, New York 10010

Text copyright © 2017 by Candace Fleming
Illustrations copyright © 2017 by Christine Davenier
All rights reserved
Color separations by Bright Arts (H.K.) Ltd.
Printed in China by RR Donnelley Asia Printing Solutions Ltd.,
Dongguan City, Guangdong Province
Designed by Roberta Pressel
First edition, 2017
1   3   5   7   9   10   8   6   4   2

mackids.com

Library of Congress Cataloging-in-Publication Data
Names: Fleming, Candace, author. | Davenier, Christine, illustrator.
Title: Emma's circus / Candace Fleming ; pictures by Christine Davenier.
Description: First edition. | New York : Margaret Ferguson Books, Farrar
    Straus Giroux, 2017. | Summary: "A girl is excited when the circus
    comes to town, but her family on the farm is too busy with chores to enjoy
    it" —Provided by publisher.
Identifiers: LCCN 2016038519 | ISBN 9780374399078 (hardback)
Subjects: | CYAC: Circus—Fiction. | Farm life—Fiction. | Animals—Fiction.
    | BISAC: JUVENILE FICTION / Animals / Farm Animals. | JUVENILE FICTION /
    Performing Arts / Circus.
Classification: LCC PZ7.F59936 Emm 2017 | DDC [E]—dc23
LC record available at https://lccn.loc.gov/2016038519

Our books may be purchased in bulk for promotional, educational, or business use.
Please contact your local bookseller or the Macmillan Corporate and
Premium Sales Department at (800) 221-7945 ext. 5442 or by e-mail
at MacmillanSpecialMarkets@macmillan.com.